P9-ELT-038
our generation®
This is Noelle & CJ's story.
Love

NOELLE & CJ™

SNEAKY SANTAS

BY

LAURA LEIGH MOTTE

ILLUSTRATED BY GÉRALDINE CHARETTE

An Our Generation® *book*

MAISON BATTAT INC. *Publisher*

A special thanks to Tina Quan, Marla Kosterski, my developmental editor, Miki Laval, and project manager, Joanne Burke Casey. Your tireless reads and sharp insights helped me write my first book. I'd also like to thank Karen Erlichman and Loredana Ramacieri at Battat for giving me this wonderful opportunity. Love to you all!

ISBN: 978-0-5784081-4-9
Printed in China

To Marla, "the best friend"
who walked to school with me every day.

Read all the adventures in the
Our Generation® Book Series

1-*One Smart Cookie*
featuring Hally™

2-*Blizzard on Moose Mountain*
featuring Katelyn™

3-*Stars in Your Eyes*
featuring Sydney Lee™

4-*The Note in the Piano*
featuring Mary Lyn™

5-*The Mystery of the Vanishing Coin*
featuring Eva®

6-*Adventures at Shelby Stables*
featuring Lily Anna®

7-*The Sweet Shoppe Mystery*
featuring Jenny™

8-*The Jumpstart Squad*
featuring Juliet™

9-*The Dress in the Window*
featuring Audrey-Ann®

10-*The Jukebox Babysitters*
featuring Ashley-Rose®

11-*In the Limelight*
featuring Evelyn®

12-*The Most Fantabulous Pajama Party Ever*
featuring Willow™

13-*Magic Under the Stars*
featuring Shannon™

14-*The Circus and the Secret Code*
featuring Alice™

15-*A Song from My Heart*
featuring Layla™

16-*Home Away from Home*
featuring Ginger™

17-*The Curious Castle*
featuring Reese™

18-*Stuck in the Middle of Knowhere*
featuring Coral™

19-*A Garden Where Friendship Grows*
featuring Nahla™

20-*A Fair Share at the Diner*
featuring Isa™ & Noa™

21-*The Incredible Ice Cream Project*
featuring Lorelei™

22-*Party Plans Go Pop!*
featuring Sia™ & Sabina™

23-*The Vacation of Hidden Charms*
featuring Dedra™ & Denelle™

24-*Finding a Home*
featuring Naya™

25-*A Love of Bowling*
featuring Everly™

26-*A Summer of Riding*
featuring Tamera™ & Rashida™

27-*The Foodie Friends Project*
featuring Rayna™

28-*Sneaky Santas*
featuring Noelle™ & CJ™

Read more about **Our Generation®** books and dolls online:
ourgeneration.com

CONTENTS

EXTRA! EXTRA! READ ALL ABOUT IT!

Big words, wacky words, powerful words, funny words...
*what do they all mean? They are marked with this symbol *.*
Look them up in the Glossary at the end of this book.

Chapter One

I'M GLAD YOU'RE NOT A TURTLE

I was headed to the mailbox, which was half a block down the street and right in front of the house with the blue shutters. Mom and Dad call it "the old Miller house" because Mr. and Mrs. Miller used to live there. I call it "the house with the blue shutters" because the colors are so pretty, like a doll's house. It had been empty for a long time. Almost two whole summers. Sometimes I felt sorry for it. Every doll's house needs a doll.

But today something was different. Today there were moving trucks and people running in and out. New neighbors!

There were boxes stacked on the driveway. One of them wasn't a box at all, but a tank with a big creepy turtle inside. What was even creepier? That turtle was staring right at me.

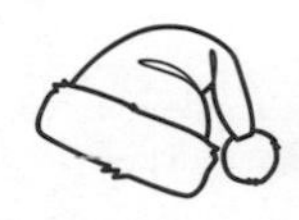

"Millie, there you are!" A very tall man came out of the house and picked up the tank. When he saw me, he gave me a quick smile. "I think she likes you," he said, and then he disappeared back inside the house.

Millie? My heart sank. My dad had said that the new neighbors were a family with a girl the same age as me. A girl named Millie. Not a turtle.

But I didn't stay sad for long. I was annoyed. It wouldn't be the first time my dad got something very important mixed up. Last Christmas I asked for a *dancer* doll and he got me the doctor doll instead. They are *not* the same at all. They don't even have the same hair.

My mom says, "You send your father to the store for a zucchini and he comes back with a cucumber." Sometimes I think Dad pretends to forget stuff because he thinks it's funny. But this wasn't funny at all. That's when I heard a voice. "Hi there."

I turned around to see a girl standing on the sidewalk. She was wearing yellow-striped rubber boots and holding a yardstick.

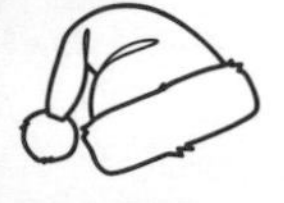

"Who's the letter for?" she asked.

Letter? I'd almost forgotten. I'd spent the morning writing it, even though Christmas is still a month away. Besides, a trip to the mailbox was the perfect reason to get a peek at our new neighbors.

"For Santa," I said. "I like to get mine in early." I opened the mailbox and dropped it in. The heavy door closed with a clank.

"What's the stick for?" I asked. I was curious why someone would be walking around my neighborhood with a really long ruler.

"I'm measuring the puddles," the girl said. Her eyes were green and her hair was dark, curly, and wild, not boring like mine.

"This puddle is only half an inch. See?" She dipped her measuring stick into a puddle right in the middle of the sidewalk. "But that one, by the curb, is four and a quarter. Must be something deep under it."

"Yeah. A pothole*" I said. "I know because I stepped in it wearing my velvet shoes. It was a soggy disaster!"

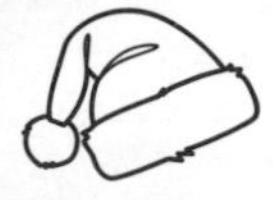

"I'll have to mark it with a skull-and-crossbones on my puddle map," she said. "Danger! Stay away Fancy-Shoes!"

I smiled. *A puddle map is a great idea. But they won't be puddles for long,* I thought. *They will be ice.* I could already feel the cold biting at my ears. I was glad to be wearing my warm vest.

"I'm CJ," the girl said.

"I'm Noelle," I said.

"Noelle," she repeated. "That means Christmas in French."

"Yes!" I was surprised. *This girl must be smart!* "That's because I was born on Christmas," I explained. "Mom says I came early by accident; Dad thinks I came for the presents."

"Is that weird? Being born on a holiday?" she asked.

I get that question a lot, so I always know exactly what to say.

"It's double the fun," I said. "Twice as many gifts, a birthday cake, and a Christmas cake. Even Santa understands. He gets me one gift for my

birthday, plus all my Christmas presents, too."

"That makes perfect mathematical* sense," CJ said. "If you just got holiday presents, it would be like skipping your birthday altogether. It has to be double."

"Exactly!" It was nice to talk to someone who understood me so well.

"There is one problem though," I added. "I only have one chance a year to ask for everything I want. If I make a mistake, I have to wait a whole year before I can ask for anything again.

"I already have my Special Christmas Present picked out. I really want this mint green sewing machine with lots of fun features I can use for my sewing projects. I love making things. But I still don't know what I want for my Special Birthday Present. I've been thinking about this for weeks, but nothing special enough has jumped out at me."

"That's a Major Christmas Conundrum*," said CJ.

I liked the way she said that. It sounded serious and important, which it was! CJ tapped her

measuring stick on the ground. It looked like she was thinking very hard.

"I wish I was born on Halloween," she said finally. "Then I'd have double the candy. And I'd be called…?" CJ looked up to the sky as if the answer were written in the large snowflakes that were just starting to fall.

"Pumpkin?" I suggested.

CJ grinned. Then we both started giggling. I knew right then and there that we were going to be friends.

I was so relieved she wasn't a turtle.

Chapter Two

TWO-TREE CHRISTMAS

"I think this one is special," my mom said, pointing to a tall fir tree. It was deep green, tall, and had a hand-written label attached to it saying, "Prince Charming." She thought it would look "handsome" by the living room window.

I gave my mom the thumbs-up, but Dad crossed his arms.

"I thought I was your Prince Charming."

Mom grinned and I rolled my eyes. Dad is such a joker.

Every year my family goes to the Santino Tree Farm to choose our tree. Each tree on the farm has a special name. The name is written on a label attached to the tree with a red string. This makes it easy to keep track of the ones you like. Unfortunately, I always like too many trees.

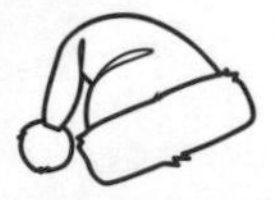

Choosing is hard.

"What about your birthday tree?" my mom asked me. "Do you have a favorite?"

Every year, we get two Christmas trees: a regular Christmas tree and a special birthday tree, just for me.

I kept going back and forth between "Ra-pine-zel," a pretty pine tree with long silvery needles and "Ginger," a stubby fir tree that looked like it could use a friend. I know a tree doesn't normally have feelings, but sometimes it seems that way! Either Ra-pine-zel or Ginger would fit perfectly in my bedroom, where we always put my birthday tree.

"I'm getting hungry," my dad said. We had been looking at trees for over an hour.

My mom put an arm around my shoulder. "It's almost time to go, sweetie."

"Come on Candy Cane, you can do it," my Dad cheered. Because I was born on Christmas, Dad likes to call me Candy Cane. He also calls me Mistletoe and Gingerbread. Sometimes it's

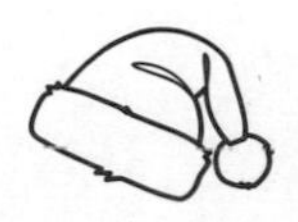

embarrassing.

"Ginger!" I finally decided.

❧ ❧

By the barn there was a booth made from old barn boards. Mr. Santino, the owner, waved when he saw us. He was helping a couple who looked about as old as my grandmother. They seemed very happy with their new tree, "Spruce Willis."

Mrs. Santino poured two cups of cider from a pot on the outdoor fire and handed them to the couple. They took a sip and nodded.

"If you like that, you'll love my holiday salsa," Mrs. Santino told them.

Mr. and Mrs. Santino bought the Christmas tree farm when they moved here ten years ago. They added their own special touches, like offering cider and selling their famous jars of holiday salsa made of cranberries, maple syrup, and a spicy Mexican pepper called "chipotle." The jars were stacked on a shelf under a sign that said "Homemade Holiday

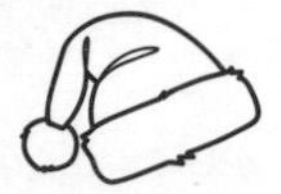

Salsa and Hot Apple Cider!"

The Santinos' daughter, Melina, was busy wrapping the salsa in gift paper with a Christmas tree design on it. Melina goes to my school. She is one of my best friends.

"Hey Melina, guess what?" I shouted. "I met my new neighbor!"

"And...?" Melina smiled. She knew I had high hopes.

"She's super-nice," I said. "You'll see her on Monday at the Fairy Mound. We're walking to school together."

The Fairy Mound—that's what we call the hill on the bike path were I meet Melina and Asako. (Asako is another one of my best friends.) I usually only have my mom to walk with me, but this time I would have my new friend.

"Did you see the little beasties yet?" Melina asked me.

Little beasties? Suddenly, I felt something warm and wet on my foot. When I looked down, I saw the most adorable, golden-colored puppy.

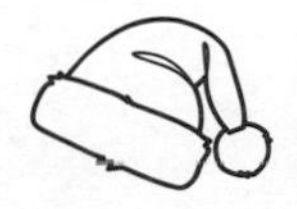

Homemade Holiday Salsa
and Hot Apple Cider!
Prince
CHARMING
Ginger

It had a pretty pink nose, floppy ears, and, from what I could tell, it had just peed on my sneaker!

"Sorry about that," Melina said.

Their dog, Gertie, had pups a few weeks ago and Melina told me that there were three more in the barn with their mother. They were all up for adoption.

"You want to look?" Melina asked. "They're so cute when they're sleeping."

But I didn't need to see the others. All I cared about was the wiggly pup with the pink nose. While my parents paid for the trees and two jars of salsa, I played with the puppy. Right away he rolled on his back, so I knelt down to tickle his tummy. He must have loved it, because he got even more wiggly. Then he jumped up on his little back paws and licked my ear. I nicknamed him Reindeer.

Melina said the name suited him. "He's always trying to jump off the haystacks and fly!"

That's when the idea hit me like a snowball in the head.

❧ ❧

"I finally know what I want for my special birthday present!" I told my parents.

We were driving home from the Santino's farm. "Ginger" and "Prince Charming" were strapped to the roof of our car.

"What a relief," my dad said. "We really were very concerned."

My mom giggled. She thought Dad was being funny.

But I wasn't laughing. I was serious. "Do you want to know or what?"

My mom turned around to face me. "Go ahead dear. Tell us."

"The puppy," I said. "I want the puppy from the Santino Tree Farm."

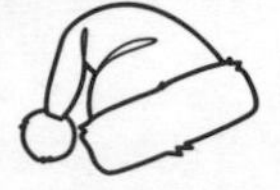

Chapter Three

A MERRY FAIRY CHRISTMAS

Our first morning walking to school together was CJ's very first day of school. When I arrived at the house with the blue shutters, CJ was in the driveway, waiting for me. The door to the garage was wide open and her mother was unpacking boxes, but she stopped to wave to us as we headed off.

"Guess what? I solved my Christmas Conundrum," I told CJ. I described Reindeer, the puppy at the Santino Tree Farm, and his adorable, wiggly ways.

"He's going to be my Special Birthday Present," I said.

"He sounds cute," said CJ. "But are you sure your parents will say yes?" she asked. "It took me ages to get my mom to agree to Millie."

I didn't think a creepy turtle and a cute furry puppy were the same at all, but I didn't want to hurt my new friend's feelings.

"Well they didn't say no," I replied instead. "That's usually a good sign."

❧ ❧

On the route to school, I always take The Path. The Path is like a long skinny park between two rows of houses with backyards on either side. Because it has lots of trees, grass, and no cars, it's safe. Lots of kids walk this way to school. Bikes can use it, too.

This morning, the grass was covered in a thin layer of snow. The snow made me think of snow angels, which made me think of The Holiday Pageant.

"CJ, I have another Christmas Conundrum I'd like to talk to you about."

"I'm all ears*," she said, as if Christmas Conundrums were the most interesting and exciting things in the world.

"Every year, the school puts on a holiday show. Our music teacher, Mrs. Fitz, organizes everything. This year, the third graders came up with a great idea. It's a little musical about a Snow Angel who comes to life to fight a bunch of angry elves who want to destroy winter forever."

"Fun story," CJ said. "So where's the conundrum?"

"I want to be the Snow Angel, and I think I have a good chance. But the problem is, I also really want to make the costumes. I made all the outfits for the Dancing Leaves in the Fall Showcase. But I don't think I can do both this time," I said.

"What if you do just one costume, like the Snow Angel's," CJ suggested. "That's the role you want anyway, right?"

"That's a great idea," I said.

There are some kids who are really smart without even trying. They are called geniuses. I wondered if CJ was one of them.

I stopped at a large hill in the middle of the path. "Here's the Fairy Mound. This is where we

wait for Melina and Asako. They're usually the last to arrive."

"Why do you call it the Fairy Mound?" CJ asked.

"I read in a book that fairies live in hills. See the hole here? This is the front door to the Fairy Realm*."

CJ knelt down beside me. "Yep. Definitely going on my map."

I was glad she didn't think fairies were silly, because I adore them. I reached into my backpack and pulled out a small box. Inside was a tiny Christmas wreath I'd made out of tinsel, colored beads, and craft pipe cleaners. I perched it on a small edge of rock above the fairy door.

"Even fairies need holiday decorations!" I said.

"Hey! You just Sneaky Santa'd a fairy!" CJ said.

"Huh?" I was confused.

"You don't know what a Sneaky Santa is?" she asked.

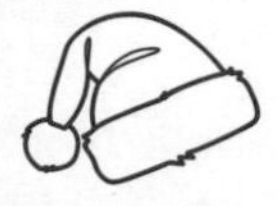

I shook my head.

"Neither did I, until my Mom told me about it last Christmas," she said. "To be a Sneaky Santa, first you choose someone to give a gift to. It's not as easy as it sounds. You have to really pay attention to figure out what would make a great gift. Then you have to find a way to give it to them.

"But here's the trickiest part: they can never know the present came from you. That's why it's sneaky. My Mom says being a Sneaky Santa is about learning to give without getting anything back, but I say it's just fun."

"What did you do when you were a Sneaky Santa?" I asked. I sure was curious.

"I shoveled my neighbors' walkway," she replied.

"Without them seeing?" I asked.

"I waited until they left for work," she explained. "I knew their habits well because I watched them like a super spy."

I wondered if CJ would want to be a Sneaky Santa again this year. We could even be Sneaky

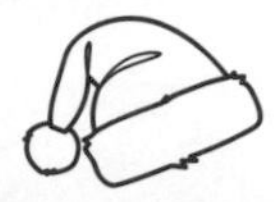

Santas together. It really did sound fun.

Before I could ask her, I heard tires skidding on the other side of the Fairy Mound. Then a bike bounded over the hill and onto the path going very fast. As it whizzed by, the fairy wreath flew off the ledge.

That's when I saw him. The person riding the bike. He was lugging hockey gear, probably late from his morning practice.

"Watch out!" I shouted after him. "You could run over a fairy!" But he didn't hear me.

"Who's that?" CJ asked.

"Only my very worst enemy in the whole wide world!" I replied.

Chapter Four

DON'T CALL ME BABY PANTS

I go to Hadley Field Elementary School. There are two third-grade classes at my school. I'm in Mr. Sumi's class and luckily, so is CJ.

I sit at the middle desk in the middle row. Asako sits on the right side of me. Henry Maze, my worst enemy in the whole wide world, sits on the left.

Henry is smart. Like CJ, he knows a lot about science and math. You'd think someone that clever could remember to bring a pen to class, but oh no, not Henry.

A month ago, he borrowed one of mine for a pop quiz and never *ever* gave it back. And it wasn't just any old pen either. It was my favorite ballerina pen. Santa put it in my stocking last year. It sparkles and writes in two colors, blue *and* fuchsia*.

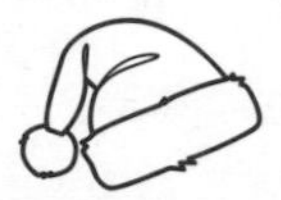

When I asked for my ballerina pen back, Henry Maze just shrugged and said, "My backpack ate it." Then he laughed. I was upset because everyone knows backpacks don't eat pens. I figured I wouldn't be getting my pen back.

"It sounds like he just lost it," said CJ when I told her the story. We were heading down the hallway to the classroom.

"I know. But he could have at least said sorry," I said.

"He sounds like a Rude and Inconsiderate Meanie-Pie," CJ said. I knew she'd understand.

❧ ❧

When we reached our classroom, I took CJ straight over to Mr. Sumi's desk.

"Mr. Sumi," I said. "Could CJ sit next to me? She is my new neighbor and it's my personal mission to make her feel at home. I am sure Henry Maze would be happy to switch places."

"That's a generous offer," said Mr. Sumi. "But I think CJ should be near the front. It will

help her catch up quickly."

"You mean we'll have to catch up to her!" I said. "She's very smart." CJ gave me a soft elbow. I embarrassed her. But my dad says people should never feel embarassed for being smart.

When I sat down, Henry Maze looked at me and said, "What's up Baby Pants?"

Not that again. I was wearing my jeans with the rainbow knee patches. I cut the patches myself and sewed them on by hand. Every time I wear them he calls me Baby Pants. I guess he thinks rainbow patches are baby-ish. Not only is Henry Maze a pen-stealer, but he's a rainbow-hater, too.

"Time for us to meet our new student!" Mr. Sumi announced. "CJ, would you stand up and introduce yourself?"

CJ got up, but she waited a long time before speaking. I started feeling nervous for her. If she had a shell, I think CJ would've climbed right back inside! I found this funny because CJ wasn't shy at all with me.

"My name is CJ," she mumbled. "We

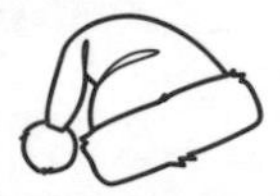

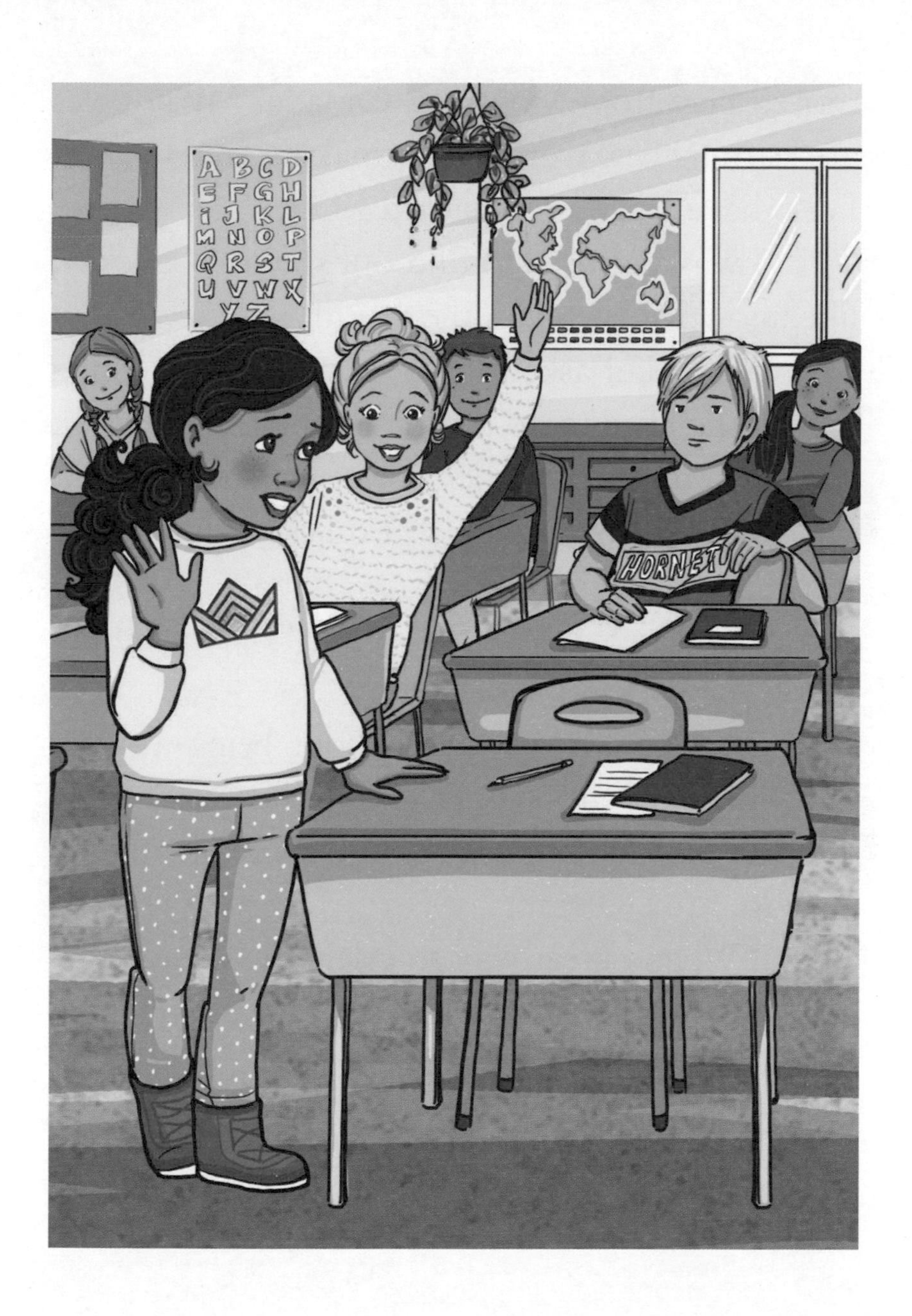
A B C D
E F G H
I J K L
M N O P
Q R S T
U V W X
Y Z
HORNET

moved here from Montreal, Canada. My hobbies are learning new words, map-making, and hockey. I also have a pet turtle named Millie."

I was surprised to find out she plays hockey, like my worst enemy in the world.

Mr. Sumi asked CJ if there was something special she liked to do during the holidays. I think he was trying to bring her out of her shell.

But CJ froze again, so I quickly came to the rescue.

"Sneaky Santa!" I spoke up. "Tell him about that!"

As CJ told Mr. Sumi about being a super spy when it comes to gift giving, her voice grew stronger and she began to sound more like the CJ I knew.

"What a great way to celebrate the holidays and explore the idea of giving," Mr. Sumi said. "How can we turn this into a holiday project for the whole class?"

"We could put everyone's name on a piece of paper and put them all in a hat," CJ suggested.

"Then each student picks a slip of paper, which has the name of the person they have to find a gift for. But they can't say the name. That's very important. Otherwise it's not sneaky."

"I have a Santa hat we can use," I offered.

CJ looked happy. Everyone thought her Sneaky Santa idea was cool and I was more than a little proud to have been the one to mention it.

The bell rang for recess and everyone started gathering up their stuff before running off outside.

"See you, Baby Pants!" said Henry Maze as he brushed past me towards the door.

❧ ❧

I love Mrs. Fitz. Some people call her Mrs. Spitz because she spits when she gets excited—and mostly when she says the letter P, which happens often when she's talking about *p*erforming and *p*amphlets and *p*osters for the Holiday *P*ageant.

In music class, CJ sat next to me in the front row.

"It's the best seat," I said, "but be prepared

for a shower."

"Shower?" CJ looked confused as Mrs. Fitz lifted up a stack of papers from her desk.

"Here's a list of all the *p*arts," Mrs. Fitz said, spraying CJ as she said the word "*parts.*" CJ wiped her face then looked at me, finally getting it.

"More like a tsunami*!" she exclaimed.

"The show will feature all the songs we've been learning in class," Mrs. Fitz continued. "Then the Snow Angel will sing *Winter Forever* as a solo*."

"That's from the movie *Ice Girls*," I whispered to CJ.

"I know. I learned it on the piano last year," she whispered back.

"You play piano?" I didn't know why she didn't say that in class before. She has so many talents maybe she can't keep track.

"Tryouts are in a few days," said Mrs. Fitz. "Everyone who wants to be involved in the show, *p*lease add your name to the list."

I marched up to the sign-up sheet.

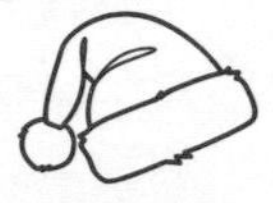

"Come on CJ," I said, waving her over.

"You saw me in class. I'm shy in front of groups," she said. "I was thinking about trying out for hockey..."

"Hockey is for Rude and Inconsiderate Meanie-Pies," I argued. "Besides, the pageant isn't just about performing. You can measure sets or do lighting or props. There are lots of fun jobs! Right, Mrs. Fitz?"

"Absolutely!" she said. "Noelle did costumes for the Fall Show and they were excellent."

"Rehearsals are after school," I told her. "If you don't join, we can't walk home together."

CJ looked up at the ceiling. She was thinking hard. "That is a conundrum," she said.

"So I could work behind-the-scenes? For sure?"

"Yes," Mrs. Fitz said, "but you still have to sign up. We can talk about your interests during the tryout. I'm looking forward to getting to know you better, CJ."

CJ seemed reassured. I knew she'd like Mrs.

Fitz.

When CJ and Melina went out for recess, Mrs. Fitz asked me to stay behind.

"Noelle, do you have any ideas for how to make the Snow Angel's wings? They have to be really special," she said.

"Yes! I already sketched out a few ideas," I told her. "Is it OK if I size them for me?"

"That'll be *p*erfect," said Mrs. Fitz, spraying me with spit as she said the "*p*." "You are definitely angel-sized."

The way she said "angel-sized" made me sure the Snow Angel part was mine. I wanted to jump and shout and do a little dance. Then I remembered what I had talked about with CJ.

"I don't know how many other costumes I'll be able to do," I added. "It depends on which role I get."

"Of course, "said Mrs. Fitz. "I'll keep that in mind."

I was relieved. Thanks to CJ, my second Christmas Conundrum was solved. I had no

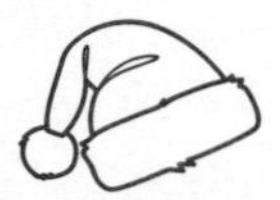

idea there would be another one just around the corner.

Chapter Five

THE EVIL FORCE

It's not fair. Just when you solve one pesky Christmas Conundrum another one pops right up to take its place. And this one was even trickier because it was also about Granny.

It all happened during Family Discussion Time, which is a problem-solving idea my dad came up with. Family Discussion Time is so family members can get together and talk about stuff that's important to them. My dad is a lawyer and believes in hearing everyone's point of view. Today Granny decided to share her point of view on Reindeer.

"But Noelle has already asked for a nice sewing machine," Granny said, as she took a sip of green tea. "Isn't that enough?" She was sitting on the sofa wearing blue yoga pants and a T-shirt with a flower design on it.

Granny teaches yoga at the community center. She says she doesn't need "material things" to be happy.

She also thinks Christmas should be about family and spending time together, which is fine, except she also thinks we should give up presents! Imagine? No presents at Christmas?

It's like she's out to destroy birthdays AND Christmas. Sometimes I call her The Evil Force.

"The sewing machine is my Special Christmas Present," I argued. "Reindeer is my Special Birthday Present. It makes perfect mathematical sense!" I thought using CJ's fancy words would help my case.

"Two of this, two of that, so many things...." Granny said.

That's when it came to me.

"Reindeer is not a thing," I pointed out, "he's a puppy."

Granny paused. "True," she said, "but what about Karma? She's a member of the family, too. I'm not sure she will appreciate a big dog in the house."

Karma is Granny's cat. She's very fluffy and cute with gray fur and yellow eyes. You hardly notice that she's missing part of her left ear. Granny rescued her from the street when she was a kitten. She's been Granny's pet since before I was born. I love her, too.

"Cats and dogs can be great friends," I said. "It says so in lots of books. Hey Karma? Wouldn't you just love having a puppy to play with?" I made clicking sounds with my tongue so Karma would come over to me.

But Karma wasn't listening. She was too busy batting a Christmas tree ornament with her paw under Prince Charming. We had just started decorating when Granny called "Family Discussion Time."

"She's old," Granny said. "She's not used to dogs."

"But Reindeer's only a puppy," I pleaded. "He's so small."

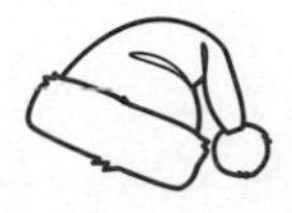

My mother put her arm around me. "Puppies can grow up to become very big dogs, honey."

I was sure my mom would be on my side because I'm her "one and only Christmas miracle." But even she seemed to be going along with Granny.

"And a big dog might frighten Karma," Granny said. She picked up Karma from under the tree. She scratched her under the chin and Karma meowed.

My only hope was my dad. I saw him looking at Granny, and then at me. Granny is his mother and he worries about her a lot. That's the main reason she came to live with us.

"A dog is a lot of responsibility," he sighed. "Maybe we should think about it a while longer."

I felt helpless. I felt crushed. How could Granny do this to me? How come I have to give up my puppy because she has a cat?

It looked like this Christmas Conundrum had turned into a Holiday Battle. Karma versus Reindeer, and so far, Karma was winning.

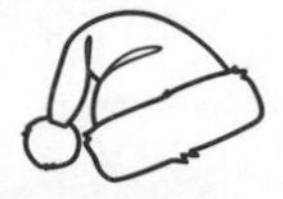

I was so upset I ran up to my room and slammed the door.

❧ ❧

Lying on my bed, I thought about Granny and how she was ruining my Christmas. It wasn't fair at all! Then something sparkly caught the corner of my eye.

It was Ginger, my Birthday Tree.

Every year my mother decorates my Birthday Tree. It's a surprise each time. This year the theme was sewing because she knows I love to make things. She made ornaments from spools of colored thread. Green, silver, gold, and red.

On the very top of the tree was a picture of me and Santa at the mall.

That's when I got an idea. *Santa.*

I jumped off my bed, walked over to my desk, and pulled out a sheet of my favorite holiday stationery. I sat down and started writing. I hoped it wasn't too late.

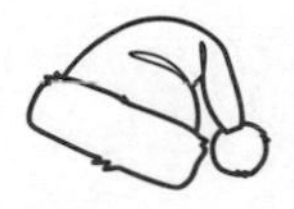

Dear Santa,

It's Noelle from Hadley Field again. I'm writing again to ask for a special favor. It's also an emergency.

I know that you can't give a living thing like a puppy for a Christmas present. For one, a puppy would be very unhappy stuffed in a sack full of presents! And I still want the rainbow shoelaces, the mystery book series, AND the Christmas doll. But I wonder if you can also use some of your Santa magic to convince Granny about my puppy. His name is Reindeer and he lives at the Santino Tree Farm. You probably already know about him since you see everything.

Speaking of Santa magic, did you send me a special friend next door? If so, merci beaucoup. That's thank you in French.

Yours truly,

Noelle

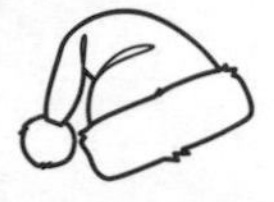

Chapter Six

SNEAKY SANTA SURPRISE

It was exciting. It was noisy. It was the day of the Holiday Pageant Auditions!

The door to the school auditorium had a sign posted to it with golden holiday tape:

Holiday Pageant Auditions In Progress.
KEEP OUT!

Students were waiting outside in the hallway until Mrs. Fitz called their number and they went into the auditorium.

"Do I look scary enough?" Asako asked. She had drawn herself a pair of black eyebrows and painted her face green. She was hoping for the role of the Evil Elf Queen who kidnaps Old Man Winter. Asako is so brave. I would never want to

look like that in front of the whole school.

Melina said she wanted to be in the Dancing Snowflake Chorus. As she danced around the hallway in her tap shoes, her *clickety-clacks* bounced off the walls.

I was warming up my voice: *Do re mi fa so la ti do*. I had to really concentrate and not think too much about Reindeer. *Would Santa get my letter in time? Would his Santa Magic help?*

I was wearing the white satin dress that my aunt gave me when I was flower girl at her wedding and sparkly star barrettes in my hair. I wanted to really look like a snow angel.

Henry Maze said "Pageants are lame," and that he was too busy with hockey anyway.

Down the hall, Tyler was juggling a soccer ball on his nose while Miriam and Dayna were spinning around in their Hula Hoop rings. I wasn't sure how plastic rings and soccer balls fit into a story about a Snow Angel, but I knew that Mrs. Fitz always found a spot for everyone's talents.

"What are you doing for the audition?"

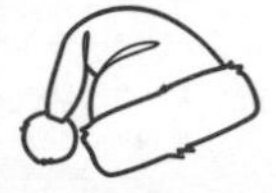

HOLIDAY
PAGEANT AUDITIONS
IN PROGRESS,
KEEP OUT!
13
20
12
18

Melina asked me.

"I'm singing the Snow Angel's song," I said. I didn't tell her that Mrs. Fitz had already given me a big hint that the part was mine.

"Number Nine!" Mrs. Fitz called out. It was CJ's number.

CJ sighed, stood up, and went inside. She was gone for a very long time. I hoped she wasn't freaking out. I started to get worried. Finally, she came out.

"How did it go?" I asked.

"It was excruciating*," she said. "She made me play the piano."

CJ spit when she said "played" and "piano" so we all laughed. I was so glad we were going to be in the pageant together.

❧ ❧

"OK everyone! It's time to choose a name!" Mr. Sumi announced. Mr. Sumi had decided to start the afternoon with our Sneaky Santa activity.

"Noelle, do you have the Santa hat?"

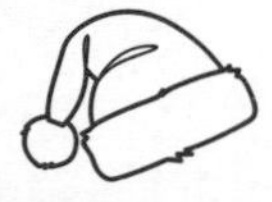

We'd spent the first part of the afternoon writing out our names and cutting them out on slips of paper. Then I went around the class and got everyone to put their name in the Santa hat. When I was done, it was so full of little pieces of paper folded up into tiny squares that I had to be careful not to drop any when I handed it over to Mr. Sumi.

"Make sure you don't tell anyone the name you chose," I added. "We have to be sneaky."

Because it was her idea, Mr. Sumi asked CJ to draw first. She put her hand in the hat and then unfolded the little piece of paper. When she read the name, she frowned. I wondered whose name she got. Probably someone she didn't know very well. She was new to the school after all. I wished I could help but that would be against the rules.

Then Melina walked up to the Santa hat and drew a name. She opened the slip and smiled. I could tell she was pleased. She practically skipped back to her desk.

Asako went up next. When she opened the

slip, she squealed and shouted.

"Isabelle Casey! Isabelle Casey!"

Asako covered her mouth with her hand. "Sorry. It just came out!" Everyone laughed. Seeing it was a mistake, Mr. Sumi said she could put the name back and draw again.

Finally it was my turn. I walked up and plunged my hand into the hat. I felt around for a piece of paper. I touched one, and then changed my mind. My fingers felt for another, then another…

"Hurry up, Noelle," Mr. Sumi said.

I quickly chose another slip of paper and walked back to my seat. At my desk, I unfolded the slip of paper. My heart froze.

The name written on the paper was *Henry Maze*.

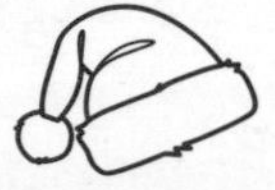

Chapter Seven

NAUGHTY OR NICE?

I kept staring at the name. What could I give to my worst enemy in the whole wide world? A can of worms? No, he'd probably just like that. Some stinky sock powder? I suddenly pictured Henry Maze opening up the gift in front of the whole class. Everyone would laugh and call him Stinky Feet. Then he'd finally know what it was like to have a silly nickname. It was perfect.

There was only one problem. Doing something like that wouldn't be very nice. It would be very naughty. Even thinking about giving Henry Maze a mean gift was a little bit naughty. I didn't think Santa could read my mind or anything; still, I couldn't be too careful. If I wanted Santa's help, I had to be extra good. My Reindeer Puppy was counting on me.

STINKY SOCK POWDER!

❧ ❧

On Saturday, my father drove CJ and me to the Santino Tree Farm so we could hang out with Melina. It was also an excuse to visit Reindeer.

I told Mr. Santino that my parents—mostly my Granny—weren't one hundred percent sure it was a good idea to give me a puppy for Christmas. But I still had hope.

"Could you keep him on hold anyway, just for a few more days?" I pleaded.

Mr. Santino said he'd do his best. That's when a family came in to trade their tree. "Greenzilla" was too tall for their living room. They couldn't even get it through the front door! Mr. Santino said he would exchange it for a smaller tree.

Suddenly, a new idea hit me like a snowball on the head. Tradesies! It was the perfect solution to my latest Christmas Conundrum: Henry Maze.

"Melina?" I asked. "Would you be interested in trading Sneaky Santas? Mine's a little tricky."

Melina looked worried. "I like who I got!"

she said. "And even if I wanted to trade, we would both know who the other person had to get a gift for. It wouldn't be a Sneaky Santa anymore."

I knew she was right, but I was still grumpy. *Stuck with Henry Maze!*

"My Sneaky Santa is a conundrum, too," said CJ. "You have to observe the person really closely. You have to take copious* notes. It's like being a spy! Remember? That's what makes it fun."

"Right," I replied. But for me, nothing was fun about Henry Maze.

Reindeer must have seen I was upset because he bounded over to me.

"When he's my puppy, I'm going to make him a pair of Reindeer antlers. You know, the ones attached to a headband. Wouldn't that be cute?"

Melina and CJ agreed. Then Mr. Santino asked if we could all help give names to some new Christmas trees that he had just brought into the yard.

"After a hundred names, you run out of

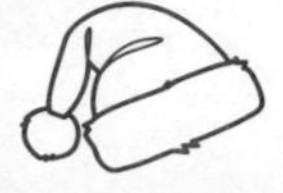

gas," said Mrs. Santino, wrapping another jar of salsa in the gift paper with the Christmas tree pattern.

Melina, CJ, and I spent the rest of the day making up names for the new trees. There was Spike, Princess Prickles (my idea) and a little baby tree CJ called Poet Tree. She said that was a pun, which is what happens when you play with words in a funny way. After that, we came up with Tree Party, The Tree Little Piggies, and even JenniFir, because a fir tree is a kind of Christmas tree.

We had so much fun that I forgot all about Henry Maze.

Sometimes the world wants you to be happy even if you want to be in a bad mood.

❧ ❧

The next day in class, I decided to take CJ's advice. I watched Henry Maze like a secret spy. I also wrote everything down on a piece of paper. I observed several things:

Sneaky Santa Observations

1. Henry Maze likes to scratch his ears. He really gets his fingers in there. It's gross.
2. Henry Maze cracks his chewing gum. It's very loud and annoying and also against class rules. When Mr. Sumi looks his way, Henry stops chewing and hides the gum under his tongue. Henry Maze is very sneaky.
3. Henry Maze wears the same school hockey jersey almost every day. The colors are yellow and green.

I wondered if I could get him another jersey. But if he had a clean one for every day of the week, he probably had tons of them. Cotton swabs to clean his ears would be practical, but also naughty because some kids might call him Ear Picker.

Henry Maze saw me looking at him. "Shake your head, your eyes are stuck!"

I frowned and looked away. He wasn't making this easy.

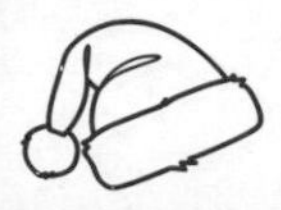

"OK everyone, it's Pop Quiz time!" shouted Mr. Sumi.

"I hope you've all been studying your holiday vocabulary words!" he said.

Other kids grumbled while pulling out their pens. That's when Henry raised his hand.

"I don't have a pen, sir."

"Again?" Mr. Sumi asked. "Where do they all go?"

Henry shrugged. "I guess they fall out of my backpack."

So that's what happened to my ballerina pen, I thought. Why doesn't Henry Maze just buy a pencil case, like everyone else? Then his pens would stop rolling around and falling out.

That's when another idea hit me like a snowball on the head.

A pencil case. Henry Maze needs a pencil case! And not just any old pencil case. A personalized, homemade pencil case made by yours truly! My dad had lots of spare pens and pencils in his law office I could throw in. I already had all the sewing

supplies and material to make it.

It was genius. It was thoughtful. It was almost too good for Henry Maze!

I felt sneaky, but in a good way. I was sure Santa would approve. After all, it's not everyday a kid gives their worst enemy in the world an amazing gift (and not Stinky Sock Powder).

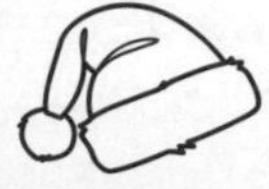

Chapter Eight

FLABBERGASTED

I decided it was OK to tell Granny about Henry Maze's Sneaky Santa gift for three reasons:

1. She's not in my class so telling her doesn't count.
2. When she sees the great gift I'm making for Henry Maze, my worst enemy in the whole wide world, she'll be impressed and think I am Puppy-Worthy.
3. I need her help to sew the zipper into the pencil case. She's an expert sewer.

I made Henry Maze's pencil case from green and yellow fabric, the colors of the school hockey team. I made sure the material was strong so the pencils and pens wouldn't poke through. Good

sewing projects are always about details.

After the main design was done, it was time to sew on the decorations. I used black felt to cut out the shape of a hockey puck and white felt for the shape of a hockey stick. Then I stitched them both on by hand, as well as Henry's initials, H. M. That way everyone would know it was his case.

"Should we add a rainbow patch?" Granny asked. I thought that was funny and we both had a good laugh. When she's not trying to destroy Christmas and birthdays, Granny can be pretty fun. Then she helped me attach the zipper using her own sewing machine. It sure wasn't easy, but eventually we got it right. My very first zipper! And all because of Henry Maze.

"We did it, Granny!" I said. "Thanks for helping."

"My pleasure," she said. "It's not easy being kind to someone who's mean to you. I'm very impressed Noelle. You really are an angel."

Then Granny gave me a big, long hug. I could hardly breathe.

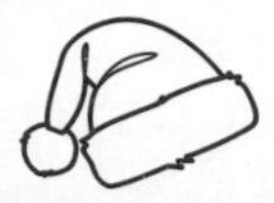

"Does that mean you'll change your mind about the puppy?" I asked.

Granny stopped hugging me and frowned. *Did I say something wrong?*

Grown ups can be very confusing.

❧ ❧

"It's up, it's up!" Asako shouted from the hallway. It was lunchtime the next day, and Mrs. Fitz had just posted the cast and crew list for the Holiday Pageant. All the students gathered around.

I read over the list, looking for my name. *Where was I? Where?* Then I saw it.

Noelle.... Chief Costume Designer and Dancing Snowflake Chorus?

I was shocked.

"You're a Dancing Snowflake!" Melina exclaimed. "I am, too. We can practice our tap moves together!"

As Melina *clackety-clacked* in her tap shoes, my feet were stuck to the floor. If *I* didn't get The Snow Angel, who did? I scanned down the list.

Holiday
Pageant
CAST & CREW

When I saw the name, I couldn't believe my eyes.

It was CJ.

"CJ is the Snow Angel?" I said out loud. *Was this a mistake?*

That's when Mrs. Fitz walked over to us. She was smiling.

"You all did a great job at the tryouts. Very *p*rofessional and charming, each and everyone of you! And what a great way to introduce our newest student. Not only does she play the *p*iano, she has a very beautiful voice!"

She put an arm around CJ. "It's hard coming to a new school in the middle of the year. No one knows who are you. Especially if you are a little shy."

Everyone nodded. Melina and Asako both congratulated her. But not me.

"You stole my part?" I blurted out.

CJ tried to explain. "I'm as flabbergasted* as you. I didn't want to be in the show. I just wanted to paint sets, or measure things, or do lights. Then Mrs. Fitz asked me what other things I like to do.

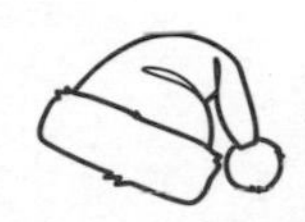

When I mentioned the piano, she asked me to play a song. Then she made me sing. I am so sorry you didn't get the part you wanted, Noelle."

But I was too upset to listen. When the bell rang, I got my backpack and headed outside where there were other kids walking toward The Path. I didn't wait for CJ to join me.

For the first time since CJ and I met, I walked home without her.

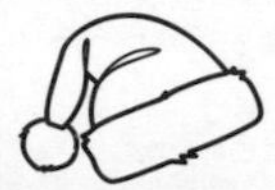

Chapter Nine

A SNEAKY CLUE

The next morning, I walked to school without CJ. And the day after that. And the day after that. Before I knew it, a whole week had passed by.

During rehearsals for the pageant, I avoided CJ. I also told Mrs. Fitz I wouldn't have time to make the Snow Angel's wings. I explained that the Dancing Snowflake Chorus was already a big enough challenge, which was true.

Mrs. Fitz agreed. She said she'd figure something else out. I watched as she walked over to CJ. It looked like they were discussing the costume.

When CJ glanced in my direction, I quickly turned away.

I felt my heart beating fast and I didn't know why.

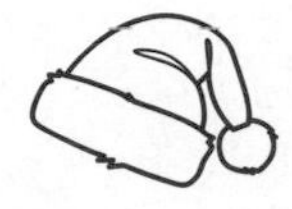

❧ ❧

For the Sneaky Santa Day, Mr. Sumi asked if CJ and I could be Santa's little helpers and hand out the gifts, since it was our idea. I knew it was going to be awkward, but there was no choice.

We'd planned our outfits—matching dresses with red tights and Santa hats—before our big fight. CJ had obviously stuck to the plan. So did I.

"You two look super cute, " Asako commented.

"We're Santa's helpers. It's our job to be cute," said CJ, winking at me. She was trying to be nice.

Instead of winking back, I just shrugged and put on my Santa hat.

To be extra sneaky, Mr. Sumi had every student in the class give him their Sneaky Santa gifts privately, the day before. He didn't want anyone to have any clues. The gifts were piled high on a big table. Mr. Sumi had placed pinecones from our holiday craft project among the presents.

"Ho ho ho!" I heard Mr. Sumi's voice booming across the room. Students giggled when they saw him.

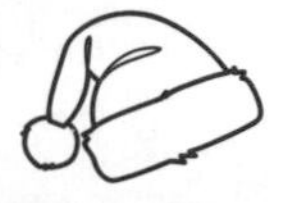

Mr. Sumi was wearing a Santa outfit. The pants were too big for him, so he kept yanking them up. He looked like a Christmas clown. In a low Santa voice, he read the labels on the gifts. Henry Maze was first.

I tried to hide my excitement when I gave him his gift. I had wrapped it in the sports section of the newspaper. Normally I would have gone for something shiny and bright, but I wanted this gift to be mysterious. Henry actually seemed nervous.

From the corner of my eye, I watched him open it. When he pulled out the pencil case, his mouth dropped open.

"Fancy," said Tyler, with a smirk.

But Henry didn't joke back. He unzipped the case. I had put a whole bunch of pens inside, pencils and markers, too. I even tossed in a pack of his favorite gum. He grinned when he saw it.

"Wow. Your Sneaky Santa really knows you," said Mr. Sumi. "I wonder who it is?"

I wanted to shout out, "IT'S ME ME ME! AREN'T I THE BEST GIFT GIVER EVER?!!"

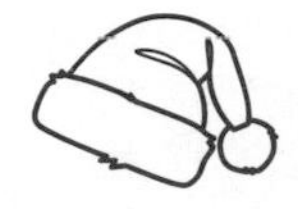

But I kept quiet.

After Henry, it was CJ's turn to open her gift—a book on turtles. She started reading it right away. Whoever got her that gift was paying attention.

Asako's Sneaky Santa got her a lip balm, in vanilla-cherry. Asako is always rolling lip balm over her lips every five seconds. Her Sneaky Santa got it right, too. I was impressed.

"Noelle? This one is for you," said CJ, reading the label on another gift.

"Me?" I was so busy giving everyone else their gifts I almost forgot I was getting one, too.

The package was a medium-sized box. When I shook it, it rattled a bit. It wasn't heavy. *What could it be?* I tore off the paper carefully and opened the box. Buried in layers of green tissue paper was an adorable reindeer antler headband!

Not only was it the perfect gift, I knew it could only be from one person. Melina. The gift was wrapped in the same Christmas tree paper her parents use at the Santino Tree Farm.

When I looked up, Melina was staring right at me. She turned red and looked down. *Yep, definitely Melina.* No wonder she didn't want to trade. She chose me. I was very touched. Unlike CJ, she was a true friend.

As I admired my gift, the bell rang and Henry Maze jumped out of his seat.

"Step aside, Baby Pants," he said.

I frowned. The nice gift I made for him didn't change his annoying personality one bit.

Chapter Ten

AN ANGEL GETS HER WINGS

When I got home from school, I went straight to my room and flopped on my bed. I thought about all my Christmas Conundrums, which were stacking up in a big pile.

What's the point of making your worst enemy a gift if they keep calling you Baby Pants? What's the point of taking a new friend under your wing, even showing them the door to the Fairy Realm, if they just steal your part? CJ and Henry were both Rude and Inconsiderate Meanie-Pies.

That's when I noticed my Birthday Tree had fallen over.

A few feet away, Karma, covered in tinsel, looked more than a little guilty.

"You!" I grumbled. Batting the ornaments with her paws and scratching the tree trunk were

two of Karma's favorite things to do when I was at school. This time she had gone too far.

I wanted to shout at her, but Karma started purring and rubbing against my leg. How could I be mad at her when she was just so cute?

As I put the ornaments back on the tree, the spool of silver thread made me think of my Snow Angel wings. They were hanging on a hook on my wall, half finished. What a waste of craft feathers. I was about to toss them in the closet when the phone rang.

It was Melina. She was calling to see how I was doing. I was happy to hear from her.

"I'm OK," I said. "And thanks for the reindeer antlers. I know they were from you."

Melina was quiet.

"Actually, it wasn't me," she confessed.

It didn't make sense.

"But the wrapping paper.... It's the same paper your mom uses to wrap the holiday salsa. With the Christmas tree pattern," I said

"I know it's supposed to be a secret, but I have

N
Sweet

to say…" Melina hesitated.

"Say what?"

"I saw CJ at the store when she was buying the antlers. It's the same store where my mom buys her wrapping paper and she must have gotten a roll of that, too. She tried to hide what she was doing, but I still saw. I promised not to tell."

I suddenly felt really dumb. The only reason I wanted CJ in the pageant was so we could walk home from school together. It wasn't even her idea to try out. She signed up *for me*. She was the generous one. Plus it's not her fault she can sing like an angel. Then, in spite of me barely talking to her for a whole week, she still got me the most adorable Sneaky Santa gift.

That's when another idea hit me like a snowball in the head.

❧ ❧

Granny was wearing her yoga pants when she opened the door to her room. I could hear music playing in the background. She was obviously doing some of her exercises.

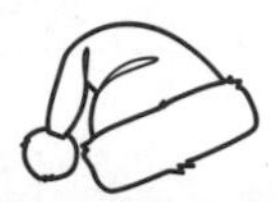

"I need to fix something," I said, holding my angel wings.

While Granny helped me sew the wings, I told her all about CJ and how she got the Snow Angel part instead of me.

"I was mean to her and now I feel horrible. Turns out *I'm* the Rude and Inconsiderate Meanie-Pie!"

"You were disappointed. Sometimes we don't act our best when we don't get what we want. "

I was surprised. Granny was much more understanding than I thought she'd be.

"But if I give her my wings, then she'll know that I'm sorry and that I want her to be the greatest Snow Angel ever."

"Sometimes the best kind of giving means giving up something," Granny said.

I nodded. I was beginning to understand some of her ideas.

Granny kissed me on the head. "I'm very proud of you, Noelle."

This time, I didn't ask if this made me Puppy-

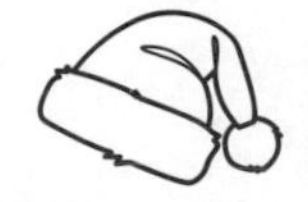

Worthy because I knew it didn't matter. Only making things right with CJ did.

Once we were finished, I went straight to the house with the blue shutters. I placed the wings on the front steps with a note, written on my special Christmas stationery.

To CJ. To be opened. From Your Sneaky Santa.

I rang the bell and hid behind the mailbox. Then I waited, hoping CJ would be the one to open the door. It felt like forever but it was probably only a few minutes later when she did. She saw the wings, and then knelt down to read the note.

I'm pretty sure she saw me because she smiled in my direction and besides, the mailbox wasn't big enough to hide me. But it's OK. Some gifts aren't meant to be a secret, especially when you want a friend to know how important and special they are, even if they did steal your part accidentally.

The next day, CJ and I walked to school together. And the day after that. And the day after that.

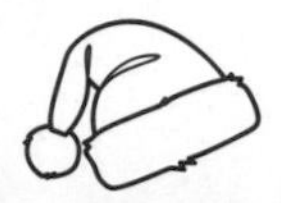

Chapter Eleven

TRIUMPH OF THE DANCING SNOWFLAKES

On the night of the holiday pageant, I waited backstage with CJ before she went out for her solo. Her angel costume fit her perfectly, but she didn't seem very angelic the way she was pacing back and forth and frowning.

"What if I forget the words?" CJ asked. "That can happen when you're nervous. It's called stage-fright," she said. "It's a serious affliction* and I think I have it!"

"You'll be great," I told her. "Plus, you're way too smart to forget anything!"

I tried to give her a hug, but between her angel wings and my Dancing Snowflake costume, it wasn't easy! We giggled and CJ relaxed.

"Thanks Noelle," she said, taking a deep breath. "I'm ready."

CJ walked out onstage.

The spotlight shone down on CJ, her wings sparkled, and she started to sing.

In a snowbank I was born
It was cold but it was warm
Your friendship gave me life
And my frozen wings took flight.

Some people say you're cold
I know it isn't true
I've seen your spirit glow
Like moonlight on the snow.

Solid as a block of ice
True and always new
Frozen in forever
That's the love I have for you.

Winter forever
Winter I'll never
Give up on you….

EXIT

When she finished, the audience clapped for a really long time. I was so proud of her that I nearly missed my entrance for the Dancing Snowflake Chorus!

After the show, the kids from the pageant, still wearing their costumes, were saying hi to family and friends.

That's when my parents joined me. My dad was holding a program* and smiling from ear to ear. My mom was crying.

"You are my little Christmas miracle, you know that?" she said, showering me with big noisy kisses.

Then, from the corner of my eye, I spotted Henry Maze staring at me. How embarrassing! He was with his family so I guess they all came to see the show. But why were they walking over to me? I really hoped he wasn't going to make fun of me in front of everyone.

"My sister has something for you," said Henry, nudging a little girl towards me. "Go on, Chloe."

His little sister was about three years old, with red hair, and a mouth smeared with chocolate sprinkle cookies from the holiday snack table. She was also holding something in her hand. My ballerina pen!

"We found it hidden in her stroller," Henry explained.

Chloe frowned and held the pen close to her chest. Henry looked frustrated. I don't know why, but knowing Henry Maze had a baby sister who bossed him around made me like him a little bit more.

"But it's *her* pen," Henry said to his sister.

Reluctantly, Chloe held the pen out to me but I waved it away.

"Since you like it so much, why don't you keep it? I said. "I have other pens."

Henry's mom thanked me, and then Henry Maze turned to me.

"See you around, Snowflake," he said.

Snowflake? I was surprised. I just got a new nickname but I didn't mind this one at all.

❧ ❧

To celebrate the last day before Christmas break, Melina invited Asako, CJ, and me to the Santino Tree Farm for a special Holiday Sleepover! We all packed our favorite Christmas pajamas. CJ's had a snowflake pattern on them and mine had little Christmas trees.

Mr. Santino had already started the outdoor fire. Little sparks flew into the air like fireflies before disappearing. Mrs. Santino handed out sticks so we could toast marshmallows.

With the barn and trees lit up by colored lights, everything looked warm and magical. Big fluffy snowflakes fell slowly and stuck to our hats.

CJ stabbed a marshmallow onto her stick, and then passed the bag to me.

"I'm going to say hi to Reindeer first," I said. "I want to try out my new antlers."

I looked around the farm. Where was he? Maybe he was hiding under the salsa table. Or sleeping in the barn?

"Reindeer's not here," Mr. Santino said. He was raking hay in the barn. "A family adopted him this morning. I wanted to find a home before the holidays. I'm sorry Noelle. I know you really liked him."

"Oh. That's OK," I mumbled. Only it wasn't OK, not at all. Reindeer was the cutest puppy and now I'd never see him again. Not even to say goodbye. My heart was broken.

When I told CJ, she put her arm around me. "Have a marshmallow," she said, handing me her stick. "And don't forget, you can always babysit Millie the Turtle. She's a very lovable reptile."

The way CJ was ready to loan me her beloved turtle made me feel a little better. (Even if I still think turtles are creepy and disgusting.)

I didn't have my puppy, but I still had my friend.

Chapter Twelve

ONE MORE SNEAKY THING

"Happy Birthday and Merry Christmas, my dearest!" my mother said, as I walked into the kitchen. She was wearing her apron with the mistletoe border and had already started breakfast. "I made pancakes for your birthday and waffles because it's Christmas. Sound good?"

"Double good!" I said. "Do I get to open a present before we eat?"

"Of course. It's tradition*!" Mom said.

That's when I heard a noise. At first I wasn't sure what it was, but then it got louder.... It was barking!

The next thing I knew, Reindeer came skidding into the kitchen. He was wearing the antlers and a ribbon around his neck with a

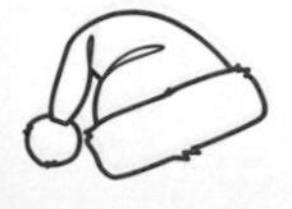

note attached:

A little Reindeer pup,
from your very own Sneaky Santa

"Reindeer!" I practically squealed. I was so surprised. "This is the best present ever!"

I picked him up right away and squeezed him. *My puppy.* He barked again, like he was agreeing with me.

Granny and my dad came into the kitchen to see what all the fuss was about.

"Well, look at that," Dad said.

But Granny didn't seem surprised at all. She was carrying Karma in her arms, who wasn't the least bit afraid of my new puppy. She was even purring!

My Christmas birthday was off to a very good start.

Then Reindeer peed on my slippers.

A Little Reindeer Pup from Your Pal Sneaky Santa

Glossary

*Many words have more than one meaning. Here are the definitions of words marked with this symbol * (an asterisk) as they are used in this story.*

affliction: *something that causes a nervous feeling*
"all ears": *listening eagerly*
copious: *a very large amount*
conundrum: *a difficult problem*
excruciating: *extremely unpleasant*
flabbergasted: *completely surprised*
fuchsia: *a bright, pinkish-purple color*
mathematical: *using numbers to make sense of something*
pothole: *a hole in a road or sidewalk*
program: *a printed booklet with information about a play or concert*
realm: *an area to live in that is ruled by a queen or king*
solo: *a song performed by only one person*
tradition: *an event that that has been done for a long time and becomes the usual thing to do*
tsunami: *a huge wave in the ocean*

Noelle and CJ helped others in sneaky ways. CJ helped neighbors by shoveling their walkway when they weren't home. Noelle secretly gave CJ her own angel wings for the Snow Angel part in the pageant. Do you have any sneaky ideas for making someone else's holiday a little bit more special?

these are **my** Sneaky Santa gift ideas:

The Power of a Girl

For every *Our Generation®* product you buy, a portion of sales goes to WE Charity's Power of a Girl Initiative to help provide girls in developing countries an education—the most powerful tool in the world for escaping poverty.

Did you know that out of the millions of children who aren't in school, 70% of them are girls? In developing communities around the world, many girls can't go to school. Usually it's because there's no school available or because their responsibilities to family (farming, earning an income, walking hours each day for water) prevent it.

WE Charity has had incredible success in its first 20 years. Together, we've built more than 1,000 school rooms, empowering more than 200,000 children with an education. As WE Charity continues to deepen its programming, it's focusing on creating sustainable communities through its holistic development model built on the five Pillars of Impact: Education, Water, Health, Food and Opportunity.

The most incredible part about this model is that roughly a quarter of WE Charity's funding comes from kids just like you, who have lemonade stands, bake sales, penny drives, walkathons and more.

Just by buying an *Our Generation* product you have helped change the world, and you are powerful (beyond belief!) to help even more.

If you want to find out more, visit:
ourgeneration.com/we-charity

Together we change the world.

WE Charity provided the factual information pertaining to their organization.
WE Charity is a 501c3 organization.

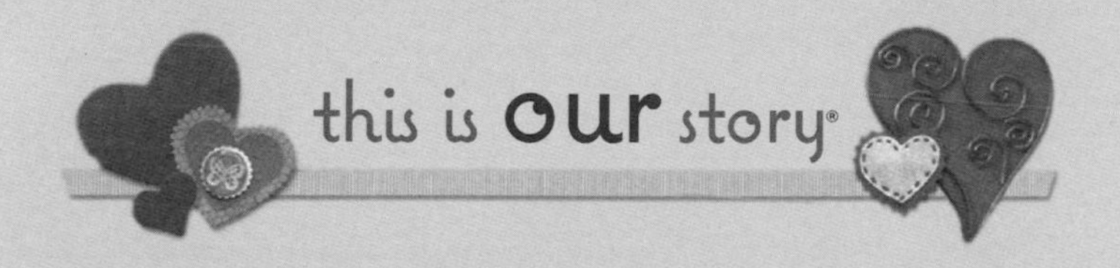

We are an extraordinary generation of girls. And have we got a story to tell.

Our Generation® is unlike any that has come before. We're helping our families learn to recycle, holding bake sales to support charities, and holding penny drives to build homes for orphaned children in Haiti. We're helping our little sisters learn to read and even making sure the new kid at school has a place to sit in the cafeteria.

All that and we still find time to play hopscotch and hockey. To climb trees, do cartwheels all the way down the block and laugh with our friends until milk comes out of our noses. You know, to be kids.

Will we have a big impact on the world? We already have. What's ahead for us? What's ahead for the world? We have no idea. We're too busy grabbing and holding on to the joy that is today.

Yep. This is our time. This is our story.

ourgeneration.com

About the Author

Laura Leigh Motte is a screenwriter. She has written for numerous children's television series, some of them featuring silly bunnies, girls who build robots, and vampire teens. Sneaky Santas is her first Our Generation® book. She lives in Montreal, Canada with her husband and seven-year-old son, Benjamin. One day they plan on getting a cat. And a dog. Hopefully they'll get along...

About the Illustrator

Passionate about drawing from an early age, Géraldine Charette decided to pursue her studies in computer multimedia in order to further develop her style and technique. Her favorite themes to explore in her illustrations are fashion and urban life. In her free time, Géraldine loves to paint and travel. She is passionate about horses and loves spending time at the stable. It's where she feels most at peace and gives her time to think and fuel her creativity.

Sneaky Santas became the book that you are holding in your hands with the assistance of the talented people at Maison Battat Inc., including Joe Battat, Dany Battat, Loredana Ramacieri, Sandy Jacinto, Laurie Gaudreau-Levesque, Ananda Guarany, Cynthia Lopez, Véronique Casavant, Jenny Gambino, Natalie Cohen, Arlee Stewart, Karen Erlichman, Zeynep Yasar, and Pamela Shrimpton.